Belinda the Ballerina

by AMY YOUNG

CAT'S Whiskers

To my mother and father

This edition first published in 2003 by
Cat's Whiskers
96 Leonard Street
London EC2A 4XD

Cat's Whiskers Australia
45-51 Huntley Street
Alexandria
NSW 2015

ISBN 1 903012 66 X (hardback)
ISBN 1 903012 67 8 (paperback)

Copyright © by Amy Young 2003
Published by arrangement with Viking Children's Books,
a member of the Penguin Group (USA) Inc.

A CIP catalogue record for this book
is available from the British Library.

Printed in Hong Kong, China

Once there was a ballerina named Belinda.

Belinda loved to dance. She went to dancing school every day and practised very hard. She was graceful and light on her feet.

But Belinda had a big problem—
two big problems:

her left foot and her right foot.

Her feet weren't a problem as far as Belinda was concerned. But they were a problem at the audition for the Annual Ballet Recital.

The judges took one look at her feet and yelled,

"STOP RIGHT THERE!"

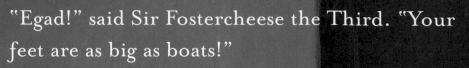

"Egad!" said Sir Fostercheese the Third. "Your feet are as big as boats!"

"They're like flippers!" said George Peach Crumbcake, the noted London critic.

And Winona Busywitch, who wrote for all the dance magazines, just shook her head and stared.

Belinda didn't even get to audition. The judges said, "Go home. You will never be a dancer—not with those feet."

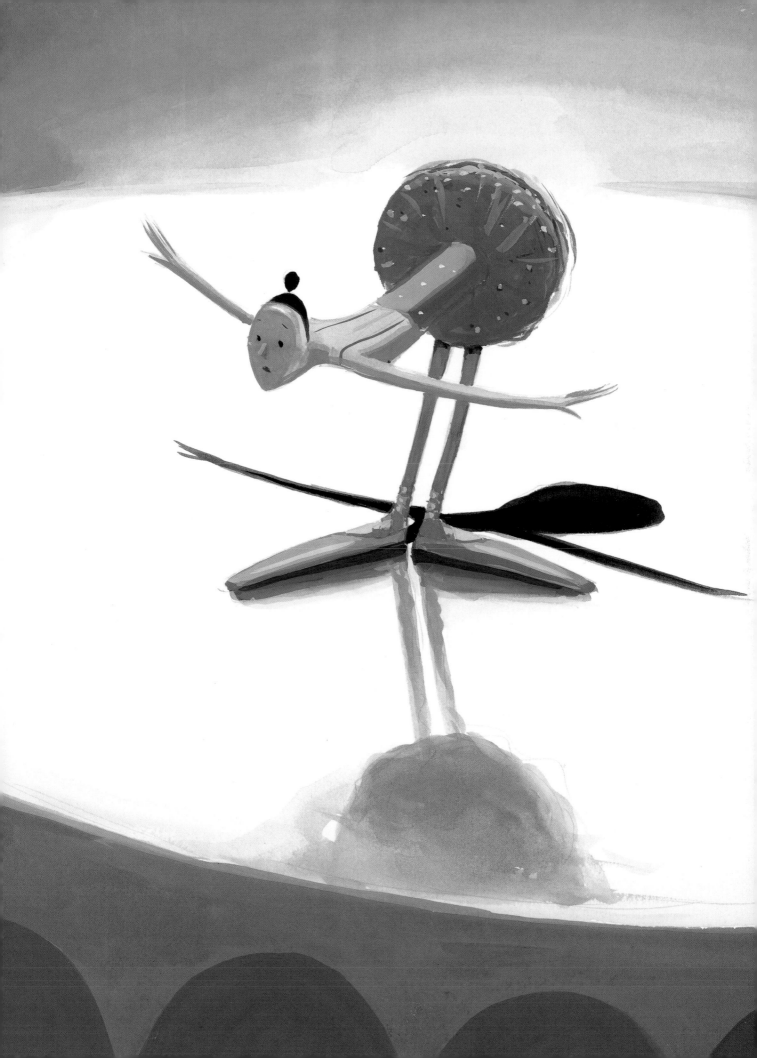

Belinda was sad. She stayed sad for a long time.

"Maybe the judges are right. Maybe my feet *are* just too big for a dancer," she thought.

So Belinda stopped dancing.

"I'm giving up ballet," she said to herself.

Since she was no longer dancing, she needed
something else to do. But she didn't know how
to do anything except dance. After looking and
looking, she found a job at Fred's Fine Food.

The customers liked her because she was quick and light on her feet.

Fred liked her too, because she worked hard.

Belinda liked Fred and the customers,
but she missed dancing.

One day a band came to play at Fred's Fine Food. They called themselves Fred's Friends. Before the restaurant opened, they warmed up with a snappy toe-tapper.

Belinda tapped her toes.

Then they played a sweet yearning lilt of a tune,
and before she knew what she was doing . . .

Belinda was dancing!

The musicians came back to play every day, and every day Belinda danced to their music before the customers arrived.

Then one day Fred asked Belinda if she would dance for the customers. Belinda smiled and said, "Oh my, yes!"

The customers were enthralled. They loved it so much that they told their friends, who came to Fred's Fine Food the next day.

And *they* loved it so much . . .

that they told *their* friends, and soon Fred's Fine
Food was packed every day with people who wanted
to see Belinda dance.

Word finally reached the Maestro from the Grand
Metropolitan Ballet. He came by for a look
because a friend of a friend told him that he
really must see Belinda dance.

He was impressed.

He was touched.

He was moved.

"You must perform at Grand Metropolitan Hall!" he cried. "Please say you will!"

Belinda laughed and said, "Oh my, yes."
The customers cheered.

So Belinda went to Grand Metropolitan Hall and danced
to the sweet music of Fred's Friends. She loved to dance!
"Magnificent!" the judges cried. "We have discovered
a swallow, a dove, a gazelle!"

They didn't even notice the size of her feet.
They were too busy watching her dance.

Belinda was happy, because she could dance

and dance

and dance.

As for the judges, she didn't care a fig!